PORTRAITS
of LITTLE WOMEN

A Gift
for Jo

Don't miss any of the
Portraits of Little Women

❧

Meg's Story

Jo's Story

Beth's Story

Amy's Story

Meg Makes a Friend

Jo Makes a Friend

Beth Makes a Friend

Amy Makes a Friend

Christmas Dreams

A Gift for Jo

A Gift for Beth

PORTRAITS
of LITTLE WOMEN

A Gift
for Jo

Susan Beth Pfeffer

DELACORTE PRESS

FOR HELENE TROSKY

Published by
Delacorte Press
a division of Random House, Inc.
1540 Broadway
New York, New York 10036

Library of Congress Cataloging-in-Publication Data

Pfeffer, Susan Beth.
    Portraits of little women. A gift for Jo / Susan Beth Pfeffer.
        p.   cm.
    Based on characters found in Louisa May Alcott's Little women.
Summary: Jo March is given a journal in which to record her most
private thoughts, but when her sisters read what she has written, it
threatens to tear them apart.
    ISBN 0-385-32668-8
    [1. Diaries—Fiction.   2. Sisters—Fiction.]
    I. Title.   II. Title: Gift for Jo.
PZ7.P44855Pje   1999
[Fic]—dc21   98-46261
                                                       CIP
                                                        AC

The text of this book is set in 13-point Cochin.
Book design by Patrice Sheridan
Cover art © 1999 by Lori Earley
Text art © 1999 by Marcy Ramsy
Activities art © 1999 by Laura Maestro
Manufactured in the United States of America
May 1999
10 9 8 7 6 5 4 3 2 1
BVG

CONTENTS

I. A Gift for Jo   1

II. Activities
    Beef Burger Chowder
      Recipe   93
    Friendship Journal Craft
      Project   96

PORTRAITS
of LITTLE WOMEN

*A Gift
for Jo*

CHAPTER 1

arch was Jo March's favorite month of the year. She knew no one else particularly cared for it, at least not in Concord, Massachusetts, where the month was usually cold and dreary, with only a hint of the spring weather that would soon follow.

But Jo believed that since her family name was March, she owed it to the month to favor it. She ignored the gray, awful days, or tried to convince herself and others that they were truly warmer than they were, or at least not as miserable as everyone else claimed.

"Days get longer in March," she said whenever others complained about the weather.

"Days get longer in January," was usually the response. "That doesn't make the weather any more pleasant."

This particular Saturday in March was a challenge even for Jo. Most of the winter's snow had already melted, but what remained was half ice and all dirty. The sky looked as though it had never been blue, and the trees gave no indication that in a month's time they would be budding.

Jo was bored sitting in the house. Running around, even on a nasty day, was more appealing than staying warm and cozy in the parlor.

"How about going outside to play?" Jo asked.

Her sisters looked at her as though she had just proposed swimming in Walden Pond.

"In this weather?" Meg asked, looking up from her mending.

"There's nothing wrong with the weather," replied Jo. "You act as though it's the middle of winter. Spring will be here in a week or so."

"Then I'll stay inside for another week," said Meg. "Besides, I have all this sewing to catch up on."

"Bethy, how about you?" Jo asked. "Why don't you pack up your dolls and bring them along? They can watch us race."

"I'd like to, Jo, but Esmerelda has the sniffles," Beth replied, holding up one of her more unfortunate dolls. Esmerelda was lacking an arm and a leg, so Jo didn't see how having the sniffles could make her any worse off.

"Fresh air is good for such ailments," Jo said. "Esmerelda is sure to improve outside."

Beth gave Esmerelda a long, hard look. "I'm sorry, Jo," she said. "But Esmerelda really isn't up to traveling."

"Amy, how about you?" pleaded Jo, turning to the youngest of her sisters.

Amy, who was reading, put her book down. For a moment Jo thought that was a good sign, but Amy merely looked out the window and shook her head.

"Are you afraid of getting your hair windblown?" Jo asked, knowing that Amy was particularly proud of her long, blond curls.

"There's no call for nasty remarks," Meg said. "Amy doesn't want to go out in such dreary weather, Jo. None of us does. You'll either have to play alone or stay in the house with us and find something to do. I certainly wouldn't object if you helped me with all this mending."

Jo didn't mind sewing and helped with it regularly. But even if she was the only one to suffer from it, spring fever had her in its grip.

"You're all stick-in-the-muds," she said. "Sometimes I wish I had three brothers and not three sisters."

"Go outside and play, then," Meg said. "See how many boys you can find. I'm sure they're all sitting by nice warm fires today as well."

"I'm sure they're not," said Jo. She took her winter coat off its peg and ventured outside without a word of farewell. As soon as she closed the door behind her, a gust of wind hit her head-on and made her eyes tear. The weather truly was dreadful, but Jo was not about to return to the house. Besides, there might be someone to play with if she just looked hard enough.

Jo walked in the direction of Walden Pond. There might be some boys skating there, she thought. The ice was still solid after a long, cold winter.

But the pond was deserted. It seemed as though the entire community of Concord had decided to stay inside and catch up with its tasks.

Jo looked up at the sky, willing it to turn blue. The sky was no more cooperative than her sisters had been. Her cheeks grew red from the wind, and she wished she could return home without fear of her sisters' laughter.

"It's their fault," she muttered to herself. Jo knew her sisters weren't responsible for the chill in the air, but if they hadn't been so set against going out, if one of them had just agreed to accompany her, Jo would have turned back immediately, out of love and concern for her. She would have turned back immediately out of love and concern for Esmerelda, too.

It wasn't fair that her sisters were sure to tease her, when Jo was the only one willing to give the day a chance. They'd laugh, call her stubborn, and rub it in that they'd known enough to stay inside while she alone had ventured out. They'd think her foolish. Amy would even call her that, and worse, simply because Jo had mentioned that Amy was concerned about her hair. Amy took criticism so badly.

Jo sat down on a fallen tree limb. *Why couldn't my last name have been May?* she thought. In spite of herself, she laughed.

"What's so amusing?"

Jo turned around and saw Mr. Emerson standing nearby. Mr. Emerson was her father's dearest friend. The two men spent many evenings together, discussing current events. Jo couldn't count how many nights she had fallen asleep to the sounds of their voices as they debated what was to be done about slavery and other social injustices.

"Hello, Mr. Emerson," she said, smiling up at him. "What brings you out on such a fine day?"

"My daily walk," Mr. Emerson replied. "It clears my mind to get out of the house and see what nature is up to. And why do I find you sitting on a tree limb on such an awful day?"

"Because my last name isn't May," Jo said, and laughed at Mr. Emerson's puzzled look. "I always feel I must defend March," she added. "The month, not the name. So I convinced myself it truly is a fine day. Only I couldn't convince anyone else of that."

"Nor I, I'm afraid," said Mr. Emerson. "I like cold days if the sun is out and there's no harsh wind. But today is the worst sort of winter's day, cold and raw. I'd be on my way home now, if I hadn't spotted you sitting so forlornly."

"I'd be home also, if I weren't afraid of what my sisters would say," declared Jo. "But I know they'll tease me, and then I'll get angry and my bad mood will ruin everyone's day."

"Do you plan to sit outside until the weather

gets warmer?" Mr. Emerson asked. "That could take a week or more."

"I'll go home before then," Jo said.

"Good," Mr. Emerson said with a laugh. "Because I'd feel obliged to sit with you."

Jo pictured herself and Mr. Emerson sitting on the tree limb, slowly turning into ice sculptures, and laughed along with him.

"Would you like me to escort you home?" Mr. Emerson asked. "I could say I insisted on your return, and thus help you to save face."

"Would you?" Jo asked. "I'd truly appreciate that."

"It would be my pleasure." Mr. Emerson extended his arm for Jo to take and helped her up.

"I'm impressed that you know when your bad temper will strike," he said as they walked back to the March household. "I'm often taken by surprise by my sour moods."

"It's when I know my sisters will tease me," Jo replied. "I've worked at improving my temper, but I don't have it completely under control yet."

"That's an admirable goal," Mr. Emerson said. "Perhaps I can think of a way that might help you."

"I'd appreciate that even more than this walk," said Jo. "I'd be most grateful for anything you can suggest to help me curb my temper. And I suspect my parents and sisters would be even more grateful!"

Mr. Emerson and Jo laughed all the way back to the March house.

CHAPTER 2

Jo and Meg came home from school on Tuesday to find Marmee standing at the door with a big smile on her face.

"Jo, dearest," she said. "Mr. Emerson came by a little while ago looking for you. He'd forgotten how late the school day runs."

"What did he want?" Jo asked.

"It's a surprise," Marmee replied. "But he asked me to send you to Mr. Marshall's store. He's waiting for you there."

"Mr. Marshall, the bookseller?" Jo asked.

"The one who sold me the Bible?" Meg asked.

Marmee nodded. "I'm afraid you'll have to

turn right around and go back to town," she said. "But I'm sure Mr. Emerson's surprise will more than make up for the trip."

"I don't mind," Jo said. The weather had improved greatly since she'd seen Mr. Emerson, and she was delighted at the thought of a surprise awaiting her.

"Should I come also?" Meg asked.

"Stay here with me instead," said Marmee. "I'm sure Jo will be happy to share her surprise with us when she returns."

Jo handed her schoolbooks to Meg, who seemed none too pleased to receive them. "I'll be back before dark," Jo said, and began running toward town to find out what treat Mr. Emerson had for her.

Jo and Meg had been thrilled the year before when Mr. Marshall opened up his shop. At first Mr. Marshall had been reluctant to allow the March girls into his store—he disliked children—but he'd soon grown fond of them and their parents. He was an occasional visitor at their house, and Jo knew how much her father liked him.

The Marches loved books, but they didn't have much money for such treats. Jo couldn't help wondering what Mr. Emerson had seen in the shop, and she worried a bit whether she'd be able to afford it.

"There she is," said Mr. Emerson as Jo entered the treasure-filled store. "Mr. Marshall, our young customer has arrived."

"Excellent," said Mr. Marshall. "Welcome, Miss March."

Jo smiled at them both. "Good afternoon," she said. "I came as soon as Marmee told me to."

"I was discussing you with Mr. Marshall last night," Mr. Emerson told Jo, "and the problem you have had with your temper."

Jo blushed. She wasn't sure she wanted her failings to be the talk of Concord.

"As it happens, I brought it up," Mr. Marshall said. "I mentioned to Mr. Emerson how angry I'd gotten the other day over the behavior of a customer."

"And that made me think of you, Jo," Mr. Emerson said. "And how you were striving to keep your temper under control. Mr. Marshall and I were both impressed by your willingness to work on your character."

"Father and Marmee have taught us to," Jo said. "Father says though none of us can ever achieve perfection, that is no reason not to try."

"A most admirable philosophy," said Mr. Emerson. "I know of many personal weaknesses I should work harder on."

"And I must learn to control my displeasure with my customers," said Mr. Marshall, "or else I shall have none to displease."

Jo remembered how Mr. Marshall had snapped at her and Meg when they'd first entered his store, and she knew he had a point.

"We decided if we could help you with your temper, it would act as an inspiration to us," said Mr. Marshall. "So Mr. Emerson and I discussed different things you might do."

"Of course there are little tricks," Mr. Emerson said. "Naming all the books of the Bible works for some people. Or counting to one hundred for others."

"I mean to do those things," Jo said. "But when my temper gets control of me, I could count to a million and still say cruel things."

Mr. Marshall nodded. "I feel the same way."

"And that was when I got my idea," said Mr. Emerson. "Jo, have you ever kept a journal?"

"No," Jo said. "Although Father has."

"Now, I could be wrong," said Mr. Emerson, "but it seems to me that perhaps part of the reason you get angry is because in your house, delightful though it is, privacy is at a premium. You share your room with Meg, do you not?"

Jo nodded.

"And in cold weather, you girls spend most of your time together in the parlor," he continued.

"Or in the kitchen, helping Hannah," Jo replied. "I do my writing in the attic, but on very cold days or very hot days, I really can't spend too much time there."

"Just as I thought," Mr. Emerson said. "Jo, you are a writer, and writers need their private places."

Jo was puzzled. Mr. Emerson certainly had no intention of building an extra room onto the March house just for Jo's use. And he could hardly expect her to move into Mr. Marshall's bookstore.

"A private place doesn't have to be a room," Mr. Marshall said. "I suspect you have a special place outdoors that you like to go to. Don't you, Jo?"

"Oh, yes," Jo said. "There are places in the woods where I spend many happy hours. But not in March."

Mr. Emerson nodded. "Exactly," he said. "In March, you need a different kind of privacy. And that is why I thought a journal might be the answer."

"A journal?" Jo asked. "But what would I write in it? I hope someday to lead a truly exciting life, but now all I do is go to school and do my tasks."

"A journal may be used to record daily events," Mr. Marshall said, "but it may also be used to record one's feelings."

"Suppose you were angry at one of your sisters," Mr. Emerson said, "and you wanted to say something cruel to her. Instead of speaking, you could take your journal and write down your angriest thoughts. By the time you were through writing, your anger would have disappeared. The very act of writing would make you feel better. Your sister would never know the extent of your anger, and there would be no tears, no apologies. Only you and your journal would know what you meant to say."

"What a wonderful idea," Jo said. "But don't journals cost money? I spend as much as I can on paper and ink for my plays. I couldn't afford to buy a journal. And if I were to use loose sheets of paper, they might get mixed up with my plays, and then terrible things might happen."

"They might indeed," Mr. Emerson said. "We could hardly have Meg rehearsing one of her scenes only to find your angry thoughts instead of Act Two." He laughed, which made Jo wonder just how terrible he thought that would be.

"As it happens, I carry quite a nice variety of journals," Mr. Marshall said. "Blank books just waiting for people to write their thoughts in."

"But I have no money," Jo said. She knew Mr. Marshall was not in the habit of giving his books away, even those that were blank inside.

Mr. Emerson nodded. "That is why this is my gift to you," he said. "Select any journal you want, Jo. Mr. Marshall will show you all he has to offer."

"A gift for me?" Jo asked. She received gifts at Christmas and on her birthday, but almost never for no particular occasion.

"For you," Mr. Emerson said. "I have my own selfish reasons, Jo. I want to see if the diary will help you with your temper. Think of it as an experiment, and of me as the scientist."

17

"Will you ask to see what I've written?" Jo asked.

"Never," Mr. Emerson answered. "A journal should be absolutely private. But I may ask you on occasion if writing in the diary is helping you master your temper. If you are willing to answer that question, then I am more than happy to buy you any journal in this shop."

"And I, of course, will be more than willing to sell you one," said Mr. Marshall. "Here, Jo. Here's my shelf of diaries. Select your favorite."

Jo walked over to the shelf and stared at its splendors. The journals came in different sizes, with many different bindings. Some were so plain that she knew she would never write in them. Others were so fancy that she would be intimidated by them. After a few minutes' careful examination, she found one that seemed so comfortable in her hands that she felt as though she already owned it.

"This one, please," she said. "If it isn't too much."

"Actually, this is one of my less expensive ones," Mr. Marshall said. "And a fine choice for you, Jo."

"Then it is yours," said Mr. Emerson. "Take it home with you, Jo, and write in it whenever you like. Just let me know if it helps you with your temper."

"I'm sure it will," Jo said, clasping the diary in her arms. It felt so lovely that she was certain it would help her with her bad moods in addition to giving her great pleasure in her good ones.

CHAPTER 3

"What did Mr. Emerson want?" Meg asked as Jo, breathless from her run home, collapsed on the parlor sofa.

"What did you buy?" asked Amy upon spotting the package in Jo's lap.

"Is Mr. Emerson all right?" Beth asked.

Jo laughed. "Mr. Emerson is fine. And I didn't buy anything. What Mr. Emerson wanted was to buy *me* a gift. Which he did, and that's what's in this package."

"Why did he buy you something and not the rest of us?" Amy asked.

Jo knew that Amy was wondering why *she*

hadn't been chosen instead. Jo remembered how jealous she had been when Aunt March once favored Meg with a gift, and felt a little surge of guilt that this time she was the chosen one. "I'm sure Mr. Emerson meant you no slight," she told Amy. "In fact, it's more of an experiment than a gift. At least, that's how he explained it to me."

"An experiment?" Beth asked. "Did he buy you something scientific?"

"Not that sort of experiment," Jo said. She carefully unwrapped the journal, taking care not to tear the brown wrapping paper, which in the March household would serve another function soon enough. "See?" she said, holding the book up for her sisters to admire. "It's a journal."

"Father has a journal," Meg said. "He puts all sorts of notes in it. Thoughts for his sermons. Ideas for articles. Is that how you're supposed to use your journal, Jo?"

"No one would listen to any sermon Jo delivered," Amy said with such fervor that even Jo laughed.

"Mr. Emerson said I should write down my private thoughts," Jo explained.

"What sort of experiment is that?" asked Beth. "Does he mean to read your thoughts?"

"No, he said he never would," Jo replied. "It's private, between Mr. Emerson and me. Until I'm famous, of course."

"What does being famous have to do with it?" Meg asked. "I must admit, Jo, I am confused."

"It's simple. Only when I'm famous will the world want to know what's in my journal," said Jo. "Think of it. All of you will be famous along with me, since I'm bound to mention you in my entries."

"But I want to be famous on my own," Amy declared. "I want to be a great artist. And very rich as well. I'll be a very rich great artist who marries an important man like a duke or a count. I don't need your journal to make me famous, Jo."

"Then I'll try hard not to mention you," Jo said.

Amy scowled. "Marmee!" she cried.

Jo sighed. There was no satisfying her youngest sister.

"What is it, dear?" Marmee asked, leaving the kitchen to join her daughters in the parlor.

"See, Marmee?" Jo said, proudly showing off the journal. "See what Mr. Emerson bought for me?"

"Oh, it's wonderful, Jo," said Marmee. She carefully wiped her hands on her apron, then took the journal for closer inspection. "Mr. Emerson confided his plan to me, and I think it's a fine one. I hope your journal gives you much satisfaction."

"I want satisfaction too," Amy said. "I'm sure Meg and Beth do as well. Don't you?"

"I have nothing against satisfaction," Meg said. "But I'm not sure how you think we should achieve it, Amy."

"With journals of our own," said Amy. "So we can write down our most private thoughts and then when we're famous, everyone will read them."

"I'm never going to be famous," said Beth.

"And my most private thoughts would be of interest to no one. I'd be just as happy not having a journal."

"I might be famous someday," said Meg. "Perhaps the man I marry will turn out to be important. Or I might be the mother of a future president."

"Oh, Meg," said Jo. "You might be president yourself, if the men in this country would only come to their senses and let women vote."

"Even if women voted, I doubt I'd be president," replied Meg. "There always seems to be too much mending to catch up on in this house. I don't care to mend the country as well."

"I'm afraid the country is in need of mending," Marmee said. "Between slavery and women's not being allowed to vote, there are many serious moral flaws in our nation. I have faith that all my daughters will do what they can to make this country a stronger and more just nation."

"I will. I promise, Marmee," Amy declared.

"But I'd do a much better job if I had a journal like Jo's."

"Jo's journal cost a fair amount of money, I suspect," said Marmee, looking it over even more carefully.

Jo blushed. "It wasn't the most expensive one at Mr. Marshall's shop," she said. "But it wasn't the least expensive one either. Mr. Emerson didn't object to my selection."

"I know you chose wisely," Marmee said. "And I'm sure Mr. Emerson took real pleasure in the giving of the gift."

"All right," said Amy. "It doesn't have to be an expensive journal. But I still want one, to record my most private thoughts for history. Just as Jo intends."

Marmee handed Jo the diary. "Why don't we make you a journal out of this brown paper?" she asked Amy. "It's very sturdy and will surely last until you're quite famous."

Amy looked at the paper. Jo knew she was thinking how unfair it was that Jo had a store-bought diary and she was stuck with brown wrapping paper.

"The brown paper is a fine idea, Marmee," Jo said. "You know why?"

Marmee and Jo's sisters all waited to find out just what Jo was going to come up with.

"Amy's an artist," said Jo, "and her diary won't just be a collection of boring words, the way mine will be. It will be full of beautiful drawings too. This paper is perfect for artwork!"

"I *am* quite the best artist in the family," said Amy. "Someday I'll be quite the best artist in the world."

"With hard work and dedication," Marmee said. "You certainly have the talent already."

"People will want to see your early drawings, Amy," Jo said. "Just as they'll want to read my early writings. If we turn this brown paper into a journal and you include drawings in it, it will last for many years. Far longer than my store-bought journal will, I'm afraid." She considered offering to trade with Amy to prove her sincerity, but decided against it. Amy was just smart enough to agree to the trade, and then Jo would be stuck with the plain brown paper.

Amy picked up the paper and looked it over. "It *is* sturdy," she said. "And I suppose my drawings would show up nicely enough on it."

"For years to come," said Meg.

"It's very satisfying paper," said Beth. "It looks as though it has a good feel to it."

"Why don't you get your pencil and draw a little sketch?" Marmee suggested. "To see if it will work, Amy."

"All right." Amy left the parlor to run to her bedroom, where she kept her drawing supplies.

While she was gone, Marmee smiled at her daughters. "Thank you," she said. "For understanding Amy so well."

"I don't want her to be jealous," Jo said simply.

"Besides," said Meg, "we love Amy and we want her to be happy."

"And I want to be happy too!" said Amy as she ran back into the parlor. "Give me that paper, Beth," she said. "I'm not going to draw anything really serious. Just a little sketch to make sure the pencil shows up well."

Jo sensed that she wasn't alone in holding her breath as Amy conducted her experiment.

"It does look good," Amy said upon completing her work. "But it doesn't look like a journal."

"It will with the help of a scissors and a pretty ribbon," Marmee said.

"I'll give you one of my ribbons," said Jo. She went up to her bedroom, taking care to bring her journal in case Amy changed her mind.

When she came downstairs, she found that Marmee had cut the large piece of paper into eight strips. Marmee folded the strips in half and tied the ribbon around the center, holding the papers in place to give them a booklike appearance.

"Here it is, Amy dearest," Marmee said. "Your very first journal."

"My public thanks you," Amy said, so solemnly that it took a moment before the rest of her family realized she was joking.

Jo wondered if her public would ever thank her for recording her thoughts. But first, she told herself, she must use it to keep from hurting others with her wicked temper.

CHAPTER 4

March became April in the blink of an eye. The raw, miserable weather vanished without a trace. Patches of ice became puddles of water and then turned into dry land. Crocuses flowered, birds returned from their winter homes, and the sun shone longer each day.

Jo, who alone loved March, decided that while she didn't love April more, it certainly was an easier sort of month. With the return of warmer weather, there were more children in Concord willing to run around and enjoy themselves outdoors. Of course, there were still school to attend and chores to do. As Meg had pointed out, there was always something that needed to be mended.

But Marmee and Father understood that their daughters needed time in the fresh air to make up for the cold winter days they'd spent inside. And whenever Jo suggested some outdoor activity, no one in her family objected.

With the sun shining and the birds chirping, Jo never once lost her temper. The whole world seemed like a jolly place to her, and she couldn't imagine ever wanting more than what she had.

One day as she and Meg were walking home from school, they ran into Mr. Emerson.

"Tell me, Jo," he said after they'd exchanged pleasantries, "have you been writing in your journal?"

Jo realized with a start that she hadn't. She'd hardly even thought of it since the day it had been presented to her. "I'm afraid not, Mr. Emerson," she admitted. "The weather's been so fine and I've been in such a good mood."

"What does mood have to do with it?" Meg asked.

"It's a little experiment," Mr. Emerson replied. "Jo is to write in her journal about the things that bother her. We want to see if that will help her control her temper."

"What a good idea," said Meg. "But Jo's right about her mood. I can't remember the last time she got angry about anything."

"I'm sure I will someday," Jo said. "I always do."

Mr. Emerson laughed. "Don't feel you have to lose your temper on my behalf," he said. "I don't want to be the cause of any outbursts."

"I'm sure it will be my fault when it happens," Jo said. "Then I'll write in the journal and tell you if it makes me behave better."

"You know, Jo, you don't have to wait until you're angry to write in your journal," Mr. Emerson said. "Tell it your innermost thoughts now. How happy you are, how beautiful this spring has become. Perhaps the journal will work best for you if it's a combination of good and bad. Perhaps you'll find your anger vanishes if you look back in your journal to happier times."

"Very well," said Jo. "I'll write in it as soon as I get home. I can't imagine ever feeling happier than I do at this moment."

"Excellent," said Mr. Emerson. "Just keep me informed about our experiment. Mr. Marshall wants to know as well. He chased two potential customers out of his shop just this morning."

Meg shook her head. "The only customers he'll have soon are you and Father," she said. "And Father can hardly afford to keep Mr. Marshall in business."

"First we'll help Jo learn to control her temper," said Mr. Emerson. "Then we'll work on Mr. Marshall's. Good day, girls."

"Good-bye, Mr. Emerson," Meg and Jo said.

"So that's what the journal is for," Meg said as they continued their walk back home. "I wondered why I hadn't seen you writing in it."

"I did intend to," Jo said. "And I will this very afternoon."

As soon as Jo got home, she went upstairs and took the journal down from her bookshelf. Meg smiled at her and left to get something to eat in the kitchen.

Jo opened the journal and stared at its crisp white pages. She took her pen, dipped it in ink, and turned the book to its first empty sheet.

What should I write? she asked herself. It was a question she was unaccustomed to asking. Jo wrote all the time, plays mostly, but stories and poems as well. She had always loved the look of a fresh piece of paper, the feel of a pen filled with ink. Words flowed out of her with no effort.

But this was different. This was a book, and Jo had been taught never to write in books. They cost too much and were too dearly treasured.

Not that this was mere scribbling. Indeed, Mr. Emerson had practically insisted that Jo write in the book. And the book existed only to be written in. Jo told herself all that, but still she clutched the pen tightly, and still no words flowed out.

This is foolish, she told herself. *Just put anything down, so the journal won't feel strange and empty.*

She could give it a title page, she thought. "Jo's Journal." Or "My Journal." Or "The Journal of Jo March." Or perhaps "The Journal of Josephine March." What would her readers want to see?

There were so many possibilities that Jo gave up on all of them. Her readers would know it was her diary. When the book was published, it would have an appropriate title.

Still, it might be best, she thought, to keep the first page blank in case she decided to title the volume later.

Having decided that, Jo turned to the second page. It was every bit as white and blank as the first.

Mr. Emerson had said she should write about being happy, and there were many things that made her happy. The weather. The birds. The promise of summer in the not-too-distant future.

Jo dipped her pen in the inkpot again. "I am very happy," she wrote in her best writing.

"The weather is very nice," she continued. *Bother! Very nice, indeed.* What kind of phrase was that? Had Jo been writing one of her plays, she simply would have crossed it out and written something better. But how would it look if she crossed things out in this beautiful, nearly untouched book?

"It's April 12," she continued. Surely her biographers would want to know when she first began her journal.

> *I am ten years old. Mr. Emerson gave me this journal as an experiment. I saw him today, and he said I should write about how happy I am. So I am. Writing about how happy I am, that is. Because I am very happy. Today.*

Jo put down her pen and read what she'd written. She ceased being happy almost immediately.

Keeping a journal was probably easy if you knew that biographers and an adoring public were never going to read it, she thought. But for someone like her, who was going to be blessed with fame, there had to be tricks involved in writing a journal.

As she carefully blotted her words, Jo made a promise that she'd learn those tricks soon enough. But the sun was shining, and she could hear her sisters outside playing. She closed the journal and put it back on her shelf. Her biographers would just have to wait.

CHAPTER 5

*J*ust when Jo was convinced spring had arrived for good, the weather turned miserable again. Seven straight days of rain put everyone in a bad mood. Jo felt it worst of all. She had so enjoyed running around, using all the energy that was pent up inside her. Now it was back to indoor activities, and with every day of rain, she got a sinking sensation that the sun would never shine again.

"Noah must have felt this way," she muttered to Meg as they looked gloomily out the window at the sodden landscape.

"Don't wish forty days of this on us," replied Meg. "The weather's been so dreadful, I've even caught up with my mending."

"I'll rip something if you'd like," said Jo. "I'm in the mood to rip."

"Thank you, but that won't be necessary," Meg said. "I'm sure someone will tear something accidentally. Someone always does."

"Always does what?" Beth asked as she joined her sisters.

"Tear their clothing," Meg said. "Which gives me mending to do."

"I never mean to," Beth said. "Sometimes I think our dresses tear themselves."

"Mine do," Amy said as she entered the parlor. "Of course, by the time they come down to me, they're practically rags anyway."

"I try to keep them presentable," Meg said. "But Jo is hard on her clothing."

"So it's all my fault?" Jo asked, her voice rising ever so slightly. "I'm the only one who ever damaged a dress in this household?"

"Father certainly never has," Beth said. Meg and Amy laughed with her, but Jo remained stonily silent.

"I'm always blamed for everything," she said. "I'm the one who rips and breaks and destroys."

"Well, you are," Amy said. "The rest of us are far more careful with our things."

Jo knew that was true, but hearing it only made her angrier. "I don't need to hear criticism from a babe," she said.

"I am not a babe," Amy protested. "I go to school now, just the same as you. In some ways I'm a lot more grown-up than you are, Jo."

"What ways might that be?" Jo asked.

"For one thing, I don't go around ripping and breaking," Amy said. "And I don't get into dark, angry moods and ruin everyone else's day."

"I haven't heard anyone else complaining," Jo said. "Am I ruining your day, Beth?"

"No, of course not," Beth replied. "But you are starting to get that look."

"And what look is that?" Jo demanded. She couldn't understand why her sisters, even Beth, were turning on her.

"I don't need to listen to this," Meg said. "None of us does. Come, Beth, Amy. We'll find something to keep ourselves busy."

Beth cast a lingering look toward Jo as Meg and Amy marched out of the parlor.

"Go!" Jo shouted. "Walk out on me. See if I care."

"Oh, Jo," Beth said. "We all love you. You know that."

Sometimes Jo knew it, and sometimes she didn't. Right then she wasn't so sure. "If you loved me, you'd listen to me and not insult me," she said. "The way Amy goes on, you'd think all I do is destroy things."

"Amy never said that," Beth replied. "But you know, Jo, it is hard on her, wearing our hand-me-downs. Sometimes I wish I could have pretty new dresses, and I don't care nearly as much as Amy does about my appearance."

"Amy doesn't care anything about your appearance," Jo said.

"I'm sorry," Beth said. "I don't understand."

"You said Amy cares more about your ap-

pearance than you do," Jo said. "And I disagreed with you."

"I didn't say that," Beth said. "Why would I say that, Jo? Of course Amy cares less about my appearance. I'm sure Amy hardly cares at all about my appearance."

"Amy doesn't care about anything or anyone except herself," Jo said. "We all know that about her."

"I heard that, Jo March!" Amy shouted as she stormed down the staircase. "You take that back."

"I will not," Jo said. "It's the truth. We all know it. Even Beth knows it."

"What do you mean, even I know it?" Beth said. "I'm not stupid, Jo. There's no reason for you to act as though I were."

"That's just the kind of mean thing Jo says," Amy declared. " 'Amy only cares about herself.' 'You're stupid.' Go on, Jo. Say something terrible about Meg while you're at it."

"You are so wicked," Jo said. "You're just a little nasty baby."

"You're calling me that again!" Amy

screamed. "I've told you over and over, I'm not a baby."

"Baby, baby, baby," Jo chanted.

"Jo, stop that!" Meg shouted from upstairs.

"And you're an interfering busybody!" Jo shouted back. "You're like a little aunt March."

Meg raced down the stairs. "How dare you say that!" she demanded.

"How dare you accuse me of deliberately breaking everything in the house?" Jo said. "And how dare you walk out on me?"

"Why should I want to be in the same room with you?" Meg asked. "Ever?"

"Some sister you are," Jo said. "Some sisters all of you are!"

"Jo!"

The girls all stopped at the sound of Marmee's voice.

"Jo, don't say another word," Marmee said as she walked out of the kitchen to the parlor.

"But they started it," Jo said.

"Not another word," Marmee said.

Amy snickered.

"I don't want to hear from any of you," Marmee said. "I don't care who started this. I don't care what it's about. This is not a household where we deny our love for each other, no matter how angry we may be. Jo, apologize to your sisters."

"But . . . ," Jo said.

"Right now," Marmee said.

Jo felt the anger surging in her. It was just like Marmee to take everyone else's side and not even let her explain what had happened.

"I'm sorry," she said, but she doubted anyone believed her.

"All right," Marmee said. "That's a start, at least. Jo, I want you to go upstairs and write in your journal."

"My journal?" Jo asked. "What should I write?"

"Whatever you want," Marmee said. "Go now, Jo, and don't come down until you're calmer."

"Why do I have to be the one to go?"

"Because I say so," Marmee replied.

Marmee sounded so stern, so unlike herself,

that even Amy refrained from speaking. Jo looked at her sisters and her mother and sulkily left the parlor. She went upstairs to the room she shared with Meg and pulled out the journal.

"I don't know what she expects me to write," she muttered. She took a pen, dipped it in ink, and opened the journal to see what she'd already written.

I am very happy. The weather is very nice. It's April 12. I am ten years old. Mr. Emerson gave me this journal as an experiment. I saw him today, and he said I should write about how happy I am. So I am. Writing about how happy I am, that is. Because I am very happy. Today.

Jo slammed the book shut. She had never read such drivel. And now she was forced to write something more. Just to satisfy Marmee. It was all so terribly, terribly unfair.

CHAPTER 6

*J*o sat in the bedroom for ten minutes, listening to the rain beating down on the roof. It was true Marmee had sent her upstairs to write in her journal, but now that she thought about it, Jo realized she did all her best writing in the attic. And although she knew the attic would be cold and dark, as it invariably was on dreary days, it still was the place where she most liked to write.

Jo tried to remember whether Marmee had insisted she stay in her bedroom, and decided she hadn't. And even if she had, she couldn't really have meant it. It was Meg's bedroom also, and what if Jo needed to stay there for hours? Meg wouldn't be able to go into her own room.

Obviously the attic was the place to be. Jo immediately felt better. She picked up the journal and the pen and quietly went out into the hallway. She could hear laughter downstairs and felt a new surge of anger. No doubt her sisters were laughing at her.

Fuming, Jo climbed the attic stairs, grateful that she had this refuge. She loved her parents and her sisters and Hannah—even in her worst moments of rage—but their house could feel crowded at times. The attic was her room, her private area, and Jo cherished her quiet times there.

She resolutely opened the journal, choosing not to reread what she'd already written. Mr. Emerson had told her to write when she was angry. Perhaps she needed the anger to write something more valuable than how happy she was over the weather.

Dipping her pen into the inkpot, Jo bit down on her lip, a sure sign of concentration. The rain pelted down, but it was the only sound she could hear and it made a soothing background as she began to write.

Today is April 26. It has rained and rained and rained. I feel as though I've never been outside, never will be outside again. I'm never happy when I'm forced to stay indoors for days at a time.

Jo looked over her words and was pleased with herself. This was just the sort of thing Mr. Emerson wanted from her. And she was sure her public and her biographers would be delighted to read such a well-reasoned and well-written summary of her feelings.

It's not that I hate rain. I don't. The farmers need rain. Father needs it for the garden. There can be no life without rain. I know that. But I do wish it would stop.

Perhaps, Jo thought, that might be enough about rain. She was certainly sounding grown-up and philosophical on the subject, but there was only so much discussion of weather that anyone would care to read.

I just got into a terrible row with my sisters.

Now, that was better. That was what this journal was all about.

It was all their fault.

Well, it was, although Jo could no longer remember just what had happened to put her in such a terrible mood.

It was all their fault. They said cruel things to me. Even Bethy was mean to me. Of course Beth is sweet and loving almost all the time, but today she was nasty and cruel. Of course Meg was as well. And Amy was a little monster.

There, Jo thought. Now her public and her biographers would know just what she had to endure.

And even though it was Meg and Beth and Amy's fault, I'm the one Marmee chose to punish. It is so unfair. Everyone always blames me.

I'm sure Father would take my side, but he is away in Boston talking to abolitionists. Father is so brave and noble. He understands me, and he would never allow such an injustice to continue.

Father would like that, Jo thought. But of course he would never see it. Journals weren't meant to be shown off. Once she was famous and people demanded to see what she'd written in her youth, Jo would allow them to. But she'd be modest about it.

Still, it was important for all those people to know just how Jo suffered. And she could tell her journal everything. There was no reason to hold back.

Although Beth was mean to me, and Marmee cruel, I cannot find it in my heart to blame them. Even Meg is not totally to blame. No, it was Amy who must be held most responsible.

Pretty little Amy, everyone's pet. She has no heart at all. She uses all who love her, and then discards them with a hollow laugh.

Jo tried to remember where she knew those words from. Then she remembered. She'd described the evil Countess De L'Amour that way in her most recent play, *The Heartbreak of Love, or, The Countess Destroyed.*

It had been a very good play. And Amy had wanted so to play the countess, a part Meg had gotten because she was older. But Amy had been right to want to play the countess. They were truly alike.

Men look at Amy and see her cool blond beauty. Can they ever see that beneath her lovely face and perfect bearing, there is no soul?

That was really good. Jo only wished she'd thought to put it in her play.

Just yesterday a boy, a fine upstanding lad from an excellent family, returned to his home,

53

shattered and dissolute. Amy had promised him her heart, had vowed she would love him and only him. But then he found her with another. And what did Amy, the heartless beauty, do when the lad who loved her cried out in misery? She laughed. She laughed as though his pain brought her nothing but pleasure.

Jo could practically hear Amy laughing. She had little trouble picturing the poor boy as well, just another of Amy's long line of victims.

And what of her family, you ask? What of the kind and decent parents who raised her and tried to teach her moral lessons? They too have suffered from Amy's wicked ways. Endlessly they weep and ask themselves what they did wrong. How could they have raised such a viper? Their other daughters, they say, have turned out so well. Meg is pure and true. Beth is the very soul of kindness. Even Jo, headstrong, impulsive Jo, is known for her generosity, as well as, of course, her great genius.

But Amy spins her pretty webs of heartbreak and destruction. She is like a perfect white rose, but one whose petals have turned to thorns.

Jo clapped her hands with glee. This might just be the best thing she'd ever written. She couldn't wait to show it to her sisters.

But this was her journal, and her journal was meant to be private. Jo felt a wave of disappointment that the first people to read her writing would be strangers who would have to wait ten, maybe even twenty years, until she was famous enough to publish her private papers.

Still, Jo felt a thousand times better than she had before. She couldn't even remember why she'd been so outraged.

The journal worked! Writing in it had made her anger disappear. Mr. Emerson was right. Jo knew she had to run downstairs and tell her family of her wonderful discovery.

She blotted the journal carefully, not wanting a single smudge to ruin her superb writing.

Then she wiped her pen, closed the book, and carried both to her bedroom, where she put them away. The sound of her sisters' laughter delighted her now. They should be happy. The whole world should be. Why, it was even possible the sun would shine again.

CHAPTER 7

"Marmee, Marmee!" Jo cried as she found her mother in her bedroom. "Oh, Marmee, you are so wise."

"Why, thank you, dear," Marmee said, putting down the book she was reading. "Why do you say so?"

"Because you sent me to write in my journal, and when I did, I ceased being angry," Jo replied.

"Then it worked," Marmee said. "Oh, Jo, I'm so pleased."

"May I pay a call on Mr. Emerson to tell him?" Jo asked. "It was his idea, and he did say he wanted to be kept informed."

Marmee looked at her watch. "Don't stay too long," she said. "It will be time for supper soon. And Mr. Emerson is a very busy man."

"I'll be back in a few minutes," Jo said. "I promise." She gave Marmee a kiss and scurried to the hallway.

"Where are you going?" Beth asked from the parlor.

"To Mr. Emerson's," Jo said. She raced into the parlor and gave Beth a big hug. "I do believe Mr. Emerson is the cleverest man in the world. After Father, of course."

"Writing in your journal has put you in such a good mood?" asked Meg.

"That it has," Jo replied. "I am so sorry, Meg, Beth, if I said anything to cause you hurt."

"And what about me?" Amy asked. "No apologies to me?"

Jo looked at her youngest sister and felt a wave of love. It was writing about Amy that had put her in such a fine mood. "My most heartfelt apologies to you, Amy," she said. "I swear I will never call you a baby again."

Amy gawked at Jo, who became aware of all her sisters' stares.

"Is this Jo March?" Meg asked. "Angry, touchy Jo March?"

"This is the reformed Jo March," Jo replied, not even annoyed by Meg's description of her. She felt proud that such petty words had no effect upon her. "This is the Jo March who knows she isn't perfect and hopes only to better herself." There. That should quiet her sisters.

It almost did. Meg and Beth certainly appeared speechless.

"Perhaps it really isn't Jo," whispered Amy. "Perhaps someone has stolen her and replaced her with this one."

"No, it's Jo," Meg said. "I recognize that ink stain on her pinafore."

Jo looked down at her pinafore and saw the stain. Meg might have had a point when she'd mentioned how messy Jo could be.

"Poor Beth," Jo said. "Poor Amy. I am sorry my clothes are such a wreck when they get to you. I promise I'll try to be more careful from now on. But first I must go to Mr. Emerson's and tell him of the success of his experiment."

"I'm sure he'll want to hear all about it," Meg said.

"Farewell, farewell!" Jo cried as she put on her cloak and opened the door to feel the cold, wet air assault her. "I shall return!"

She raced out of the house, no longer caring what her sisters were saying. What difference did it make? The important thing was, she felt fine.

Mr. Emerson lived in a house almost as grand as Aunt March's, but Jo never felt the dread she knew in her calls on Aunt March. Visiting Mr. Emerson was a treat. She had called on him by herself only a handful of times, when he had invited her to borrow a book from his splendid library. He practically did support Mr. Marshall's bookshop single-handedly.

She knocked on the door and was delighted when Mr. Emerson himself opened it.

"Why, Jo," he said. "What brings you out on such a dreary day?"

"I simply had to tell you," Jo said. "I was in a horrible mood, and Marmee made me write in the journal."

"This is interesting," Mr. Emerson said. "Come in, Jo, and warm yourself by the fire as you inform me of how our experiment is working."

Jo gratefully accepted Mr. Emerson's invitation. His house was warm and comfortable, especially after the walk through the rain.

Mr. Emerson rang for a servant and requested some tea. He led Jo to his library, a room Jo regarded as the most perfect in the world. It was filled with endless shelves lined with books, including many Mr. Emerson had written.

"Sit by the fire," Mr. Emerson suggested. The servant appeared almost magically, carrying a tray with a teapot, teacups, and a plate of gingersnaps.

Jo took a sip of tea and nibbled a gingersnap. She hadn't realized how hungry she was until she saw the cookies, but she reminded herself that supper would be waiting for her when she got home. Besides, it wouldn't be right to devour all the cookies Mr. Emerson was kind enough to offer.

"So you wrote in your journal," Mr. Emerson said. "Were you angry when you began?"

"Terribly," Jo said, feeling so warm and contented it was nearly impossible to recollect ever having been angry. "My sisters had been saying cruel things to me. They do, you know. Amy in particular, even though she seems so sweet."

Mr. Emerson nodded. "Appearances can be deceiving," he said. "Have another gingersnap, Jo."

"Thank you," Jo said, cheerfully helping herself. "And Marmee. She is the best mother in the world, but today I suppose the rain affected her too. She failed to see that I was blameless. Instead she took my sisters' side."

"Poor Jo."

Jo nodded. "Don't hold it against Marmee. She's as close to perfect as a mother can be."

"Your mother is one of the finest people I know," Mr. Emerson said. "But after a week of rain, no one is perfect."

"How right you are," Jo said. "Anyway, Marmee told me to write in my journal. I must admit I was too angry at the injustices I'd endured to think of it myself. I went to my room and got the journal, and then I went to the attic. I do all my best work in the attic. Perhaps Father told you about my most recent play, *The Heartbreak of Love, or, The Countess Destroyed*? I wrote it there."

"Your father frequently tells me of your literary work," Mr. Emerson said. "Although I cannot say for sure that he told me of that particular one."

"It's one of my best," Jo said. "Everyone who saw it agrees. But the point is, I wrote in my journal, and the more I wrote, the happier I became. I'm so happy now, I can't even remember why I was angry in the first place. Do you ever get really, dreadfully angry, Mr. Emerson? I can't imagine how anyone who has a room this fine ever could."

Mr. Emerson laughed. "I certainly do. Even kings get angry, Jo. Especially kings, I might say."

Jo nodded. "I know wealth does not guarantee happiness," she said. "But if I'm to be happy, I'd just as soon be wealthy as well."

"Well put," said Mr. Emerson. He smiled. "I must ask your father to invite me the next time there is a performance of one of your plays. If you wouldn't mind my attending, that is."

"I should be delighted," Jo said, and took a final sip of her tea. "Now I really must be going."

"I'll get the gingersnaps wrapped for you to take home," Mr. Emerson said. "Your sisters would most likely enjoy the treat."

"They'd love it," Jo said, happy to have something to share with her sisters. "That's very kind of you, Mr. Emerson."

"I'm just pleased our experiment is working out so well," Mr. Emerson replied. "Mr. Marshall will be happy also, although I don't know if he'd ever be able to make his most annoying customers wait while he goes off to the back to confide in a journal."

"That would be a challenge," Jo agreed. She lingered as the servant took the plate of gingersnaps, then returned with them in a linen-covered basket.

"I'll bring the basket back tomorrow," Jo promised.

"I look forward to seeing you then," said Mr. Emerson as he escorted her to the front door.

The rain had stopped, and as Jo and Mr. Emerson stood outside, they saw a rainbow arch across the sky.

"Oh, Mr. Emerson," Jo said. "Isn't it beautiful?"

"It is indeed, Jo," replied Mr. Emerson. "It's truly an unexpected gift."

CHAPTER 8

*A*s soon as she was out of Mr. Emerson's sight, Jo paused to count the cookies in the basket. There were a dozen. Two each for her, Meg, Beth, Amy, Marmee, and Hannah, Jo calculated. It was a shame her father wasn't home to enjoy them as well, but twelve didn't divide nearly as neatly by seven as it did by six.

And although it was true Jo had already eaten two of the delicious cookies at Mr. Emerson's, if she sacrificed her next two, then twelve would have to be divided by five, and that was as awkward as seven. She was sure her sisters wouldn't mind that she got four cookies to their two. In fact, to make sure of it, she would keep her good fortune to herself.

The road between Mr. Emerson's house and the Marches' was muddy and filled with puddles. Jo knew she tended to be careless when it came to clothing, but today she took special care to watch where she walked and to keep her shoes and clothing free of spatters. Her parents had taught her to be considerate of others, and Beth and Amy deserved clothes as nice as those Jo had.

I am custodian of their clothing, Jo told herself as she swerved to avoid a three-foot puddle she might otherwise have tried to jump over. She felt quite righteous and very grown-up by the time she got home.

"I'm back!" she sang as she opened the door. "And I've brought a special treat for us all."

Silence greeted her announcement. Jo knew immediately that it wasn't a happy silence.

"Where is everyone?" she asked, her voice suddenly lower. "Is everything all right?"

"We're upstairs, Jo," called Marmee.

Jo put the gingersnaps on the dining room table and climbed the stairs. Something dreadful had happened, she just knew it.

"Is everyone all right?" she asked, terrified of what she would find. She could hear sobbing coming from Beth and Amy's room, so she ran there. She didn't know how she could bear it if one of them had been hurt.

Amy was lying on the bed, crying her heart out. Marmee was holding her while Meg and Beth stood by. Jo couldn't make out their expressions and didn't bother trying. Instead she raced to her youngest sister's side and knelt down to take Amy's hand.

"Amy, you poor darling," she said. "What happened? Are you all right?"

Amy looked up at Jo and burst into even more hysterical sobs. "Go away!" she shouted. "I never want to see you again!"

"Does she have a fever?" Jo asked, pulling back from Amy's bedside. "Have you called for the doctor?"

"She has no fever," Meg said, her voice cold

as the March wind. "She knows just what she is saying."

"Jo, how could you?" Beth asked, her voice filled with quiet reproach.

"How could I what?" Jo asked. In her confusion, she thought her sisters were upset about the gingersnaps she'd already eaten. But they couldn't possibly know. "How could I what?" she repeated, looking down at her cloak, her dress, her shoes, which she'd taken such care to keep tidy. She'd done nothing. She hadn't even been home. And yet her sisters were blaming her again.

"The names!" Amy cried. "Those awful names!"

Amy could carry on, Jo knew. Little things could set her off, much as little things could enrage Jo. But Amy's pain was obviously real this time, and Jo felt a stab of guilt, even though she had no idea what she was supposed to have done.

"What awful names?" Jo asked. "Marmee, what is going on?"

" 'Viper,' " Meg said. " 'Heartless.' 'Without a soul.' "

"Who would call Amy such terrible things?" Jo asked. "Show him to me, and I'll defend Amy's name and honor."

Even Amy stopped sobbing. Jo felt the eyes of those she loved best turning to her in shock.

"What?" Jo asked. "Was it a friend of mine? If it was, I'll never speak to him again."

"Jo," Beth said in a gentle, almost pitying voice. "Jo, *you* called Amy those names."

"Never," Jo said. "All I called her was a baby. And I vowed never to call her that again." She racked her brain to think of other terrible names she might have called Amy. When she was angry, she knew, she said wretched things. But surely she'd never called Amy a heartless viper.

Amy began crying again. Marmee stroked her beautiful blond curls. As she did, Meg silently handed Jo a book.

"What's this?" Jo asked. "My journal?"

"Your journal," Meg said. "In which you described your most intimate thoughts. In which you wrote what you truly thought of us."

"I don't mind that you thought me mean," Beth said. "Perhaps I was mean, although I certainly didn't intend to be. But you never should have written that Amy has no soul."

"It's bad enough you called her a little monster," Meg added. "That is just the sort of thing you do call her when you get into one of your rages. We're used to abuse of that nature from you. But really, Jo. To call her soulless, a viper. Have you no shame at all?"

"Amy is a good girl," Beth said. "Her soul is beautiful and pure."

"I'm sorry," Jo said. "Of course Amy has a beautiful soul."

"Then why did you write such awful things about me?" Amy asked, wiping away her tears.

"I don't know," Jo said. She looked at her sisters' accusing faces and wished she had never returned home. "I just wrote what came to my mind. Wasn't that what I was supposed to do, Marmee?"

"I suppose," Marmee said. "I simply didn't think your words would be so hurtful."

"I never meant them to be," Jo said. No one, not even Beth, looked likely to forgive her.

Jo looked down at the journal. An hour ago, she had thought it her savior. Now it had betrayed her. She opened it to the pages she'd written and saw a tearstain on one of them.

"Wait a second," she said. "If you know what I wrote, then that means you read my journal. Which one of you did that?"

"I did," Amy said, looking as though she was about to begin crying all over again.

"How dare you?" Jo shrieked. "How dare you read my most private and personal thoughts!"

"How dare you write them!" Amy shot back.

"I'll write whatever I want!" Jo shouted. "You had no right to read this. And then, to make things worse, you let the others read it too."

"She was so upset," Beth said. "We had to see why she was crying so."

"She was crying because she's an interfering, nosy little baby monster," Jo said, forgetting all her vows of an hour past. "How dare she? How dare any of you? Marmee, how could you let them?"

"I didn't encourage anyone to read your journal, Jo," Marmee said. "And I certainly don't condone such behavior, but what's done is done."

"This is too much," Jo said, clutching her journal. "I am teased and tormented, and now even my most basic privacy is invaded. Cry your silly tears, Amy. What you read is nothing compared to what you truly are."

*B*eth was the first one to climb the attic stairs after Jo had run from her family. "Jo," she said in her soft and loving voice. "May I come in?"

"You *are* in," Jo said, but seeing her sister's stricken look, she changed her own expression. "Bethy, I'm sorry," she said. "I never meant to hurt your feelings."

"I know that," Beth said. "You did make me feel stupid earlier, but sometimes I get confused and my words don't always come out right. That's one reason why it frightens me so to speak to strangers."

"You should never be frightened," Jo said.

"There isn't a person in the world as dear as you, or as good. Strangers should be honored when you speak to them."

Beth giggled. "I'll tell them so the next time I meet them," she said. "Jo, I'm sorry I looked at your journal. Amy was so upset, I simply didn't think about what I was doing."

"Amy has a gift for making people forget what they're doing," Jo said. "She thinks the sun and moon revolve around her. No, she demands that the sun and moon revolve around her, and then they do."

"She's just a little girl," Beth said. "It can't be easy for her, with all of us treating her like a baby. If she demands that the sun and moon revolve around her, it's because she feels so much that she revolves around us. It's true, Jo. She talks to me at night before we go to sleep, just as I'm sure you and Meg talk to each other."

Jo thought of all the confidences she and Meg had shared in their bedroom. "I never thought of you and Amy talking like that," she admitted.

"Jo, you don't think of Amy at all," Beth said. "Except when she's annoying you."

"I think of her," Jo said. "I cast her in my plays."

"Because she demands it," said Beth. "Amy is sure the only way she can get any attention from you is if she jumps up and down right under your nose. And even then you mostly look down at her and call her a baby. Would you like it if that were the only way Meg paid attention to you?"

"No," Jo said. "But Amy really can be a little monster."

"She can be difficult," Beth admitted. "So can you, Jo. But we love you both and put up with it."

Jo thought about how upset she'd been when she feared Amy was hurt. Still, she remained angry that Amy had read her journal.

"She had no right to do what she did," Jo said. "None. She never gives any thought to what's right or wrong."

"I'm not defending Amy for reading your journal," Beth said. "She was wrong to do so, and she owes you an apology. But, Jo, I don't want you to get into one of your rages. I was so proud of you today when you came downstairs all smiling and happy. Sometimes it takes days for you to become yourself again, and today you calmed down quickly, thanks to your journal. I thought of how delighted Mr. Emerson would be, and Father, too, when he returns from Boston."

"Father would understand what a great wrong Amy did," Jo said. "He always tells us to respect each other."

"Yes, he does," Beth said. "But maybe Amy doesn't think you respect her. Do you, Jo?"

Jo had no chance to answer because Marmee called her downstairs.

"I must go," Jo said. As she rose, she gave Beth a kiss. "You are so good. If I could be half as good as you, I'd be a hundred times better a person."

"You are that good," Beth said. "Sometimes you just don't allow yourself to be."

Jo wondered what Beth meant, but knew from Marmee's tone that she must go downstairs immediately. She raced down the attic stairs, looked in her bedroom and in Amy's, and, not finding Marmee there, went to the first floor in search of her.

"Your mother's in her bedroom," Hannah told her as Jo peeked into the kitchen. "You'd best be going in there right away."

"Thank you," Jo said. She remembered how pretty Marmee had looked, bent over her reading earlier that day. She thought of how loving Marmee had been to Amy, stroking her head, comforting the weeping child.

Beth's gotten the best of Marmee, Jo thought. *And I've gotten the worst.*

"Thank you for coming so promptly, Jo," Marmee said as Jo entered her bedroom. "Amy is here with me. I thought it best if we all spoke in private."

Jo nodded. She couldn't really say she was surprised to see Amy by Marmee's side.

"I love my daughters very much," Marmee said. "But I am under no illusion that any of them is perfect."

"I know I'm not," Jo said. "And even if I

didn't know, everyone takes great pleasure in informing me."

"No one is teased as much as I am," Amy said. "You all torment me all the time."

"You are both sinned against and sinning," Marmee said. "We are in complete agreement about that. But the important thing is that the two of you examine the way you treat each other. Until you do, there will never be peace in this household."

Jo looked at her youngest sister's face. She wasn't a baby, Jo realized. Not anymore. But she was young and deserving of protection. Jo suspected Beth had been right when she said Amy felt the only way she could get attention from Jo was by jumping up and down under her nose.

"I do tease you, Amy," Jo said. "But you provoke me."

"You make me so angry," Amy replied. "You never seem to know I'm around unless it's to make fun of me."

"I wonder if the two of you have any idea how much alike you are," Marmee said.

"You're both headstrong, talented, very clever, and very willful. Jo gets angry. Amy weeps. You both feel things so deeply, and neither of you has enough control over your emotions. It's no wonder you get on each other's nerves. I would never ask you to be the best of friends. That will come in time as you learn how important a sister's love can be. But you cannot deliberately hurt each other. I won't allow that."

Jo looked down at her feet and thought how hard she'd tried not to get mud on her shoes, knowing they would someday be Amy's. "I do love Amy," she said. "And I do forget sometimes that she isn't a baby anymore. She gets better and better in my plays. She's more fun to do things with. And I marvel at her drawings. But she still shouldn't have read my journal."

Amy was silent. "I know," she said finally. "I was just so curious. I haven't put a thing in my journal and there you were, so happy after you'd written in yours. I thought if I could just see what you wrote, maybe I'd know what to write in mine. I want to be famous too, Jo. Just as much as you do."

"That's right," Marmee said. "That is another thing you two have in common. You are both ambitious."

"The things I wrote," Jo said, "about your being a viper, without a soul—they weren't about you. You must have known that, Amy. They were about some made-up girl, like the Countess De L'Amour. I just got to writing and the next thing I knew, I was having the most wonderful time making things up." She paused. "Perhaps I shouldn't keep a journal," she said. "Perhaps I should limit myself to fiction. That seems to be what I write even if I don't intend to."

"I didn't mind the part about being beautiful," Amy said. "Was that part fiction, Jo?"

Jo looked at her little sister. She saw a seven-year-old with a tear-stained face and tousled hair. "You're very beautiful," she said.

Amy smiled. "I love you, Jo. And I really

am sorry I read your journal. I'll never do that again. I promise."

"That will be an easy promise for you to keep," Jo said. "I think I've learned enough from journal writing to be sure I'll never keep one again!"

C H A P T E R   1 0

"Do you want to go to Mr. Marshall's store with me?" Jo asked Meg after school a few days later. "Father asked me to pick up a book for him."

"I don't think so," Meg said. "It looks as if it might rain again. I think I'll go straight home."

"I'll see you there, then." Jo waved good-bye to her sister and began the short walk to Mr. Marshall's bookstore.

When she arrived, she was pleased to see Mr. Emerson there.

"Hello, Jo," Mr. Emerson said. "We were just talking about you."

"You were?" Jo asked.

"I was telling Mr. Marshall about your great success with the journal," Mr. Emerson replied. "We were praising ourselves for our cleverness in thinking of it."

"It wasn't so great a success after all," Jo said. "As a matter of fact, I've decided never to write in it again."

"Why is that?" Mr. Marshall asked. "From what Mr. Emerson told me, it changed your bad mood into a good one."

"It did," Jo said. "But it wasn't because I poured my soul into it. I just began to make up a character, the same way I do for my plays. My journal simply became a story."

"Indeed," Mr. Emerson said. "That's interesting as well. It never occurred to me that you'd be writing fiction."

"Was it good fiction?" Mr. Marshall asked. "Should I reserve a space on my shelves for it?"

Jo blushed. Then she sensed how Amy must feel when Jo said such things to her.

"I'll be a published writer someday," she

said. "When I am, I'll be sure to tell you, Mr. Marshall."

"I suspect you're right," Mr. Emerson said. "Only a true writer could go from angry to happy by making up a character. We have a novelist on our hands here, Mr. Marshall, and we should treat her accordingly."

"A local author of popular novels could only do my store good," Mr. Marshall declared. "Then all those twittering women who drive me mad will have something to buy from me."

"More popular fiction and fewer scholarly works," Mr. Emerson said. "That sounds like an excellent formula for success in a bookstore, although perhaps not as appealing a store as I might like."

"I'll keep it in mind," Mr. Marshall said. "In the meantime, I'm disappointed. I'd been hoping, Jo, that you would lead me from anger to a better control of my emotions. But I know I'm not a born writer. I enjoy reading about fictional characters but have no desire to create any."

"We might still learn from Jo," said Mr. Emerson. "Perhaps if we could determine what causes Jo's angry spells, we could figure out a cure that would work for both of you."

Jo thought about it. "My sisters make me angry," she said.

"I have no sisters," Mr. Marshall said.

"Bad weather," Jo said. "I noticed that this spring, I was much more likely to get into a rage when it was cold or rainy than in nice weather."

"Weather has no effect upon me," Mr. Marshall said. "In fact, I'm hardly aware of it, I work so hard in the shop."

"Then I don't think I can help you," Jo said. "Those are the things that make me angry most often."

"But there must be other things as well," said Mr. Marshall. "Irritating customers?"

"Jo is ten," Mr. Emerson pointed out. "She has no customers."

"Irritating people, then," Mr. Marshall said. "Surely they disturb you, Jo?"

"Aunt March does," Jo admitted.

Mr. Marshall shook his head. "Mrs. March is one of my best customers," he said. "She always knows just what she wants and never quibbles about the price."

"Sometimes I get angry because I want more than I can have," Jo said. "Does that ever happen to you, Mr. Marshall?"

"Indeed it does!" he exclaimed. "I think sometimes my entire life is a protest against what I do not have."

"Very well," said Mr. Emerson. "Envy and greed motivate you both."

"Oh, dear," Jo said. "Envy and greed are sins, aren't they?"

"They're certainly not virtues," Mr. Emerson said.

Jo sighed. "Life would be so much easier if I were perfect," she said.

Mr. Emerson laughed. "Life might be easier, but you'd be less delightful. Come, Jo. Let me escort you home before the rain, which Mr. Marshall won't notice, falls on both our heads."

"Thank you." Jo began to leave the store

before she remembered why she'd come. "My father's book," she said to Mr. Marshall. "Has it arrived yet?"

"Yes, it has," Mr. Marshall said. "I almost forgot to give it to you."

"So you're both forgetful as well," Mr. Emerson said. "It's a good thing for all of us that forgetfulness isn't a sin."

Jo took the book from Mr. Marshall and thanked him. She smiled as Mr. Emerson extended his arm to her, a gentleman's gesture to a lady. She was imperfect, horribly imperfect. But it was good to know she was also truly a writer. Being one was the best gift she could imagine.

PORTRAITS OF
LITTLE WOMEN
ACTIVITIES

BEEF BURGER CHOWDER

*Nothing tastes as good as a hearty bowl of chowder
on a cold winter night.*

INGREDIENTS

2 medium potatoes
1 large carrot
2 stalks celery
1 medium onion
1 small bunch curly or flat-leaf parsley
2 medium cloves garlic
2 tablespoons olive oil or other vegetable oil

1 pound very lean ground beef (or ground
  turkey or veal)
2 quarts water
3 cubes beef bouillon
1 medium can diced tomatoes
8 ounces fine egg noodles (or 1 cup barley or
  other small fine pasta)

1. Peel and dice potatoes and carrot. Set aside
   in cold water.
2. Dice celery and onion.
3. Chop parsley and garlic finely.
4. Heat 2 tablespoons of oil in skillet. Add
   onions, garlic, and celery and about 2
   tablespoons of the parsley. Sauté until
   tender.
5. Add the beef (or other meat of choice) and
   brown lightly.
6. Let meat and onion mixture cool. Discard all
   fat.
7. Add water to a 3- or 4-quart covered pot
   and bring to a boil. Add the bouillon,
   potatoes, and carrots and cook, covered,
   until tender.
8. Add meat-and-onion mixture and diced
   tomatoes. Lower to medium heat and allow
   to simmer, covered, for at least 30 minutes.

9. Add egg noodles (or other pasta of choice) and cook until tender.
10. Add remaining parsley and cook another 5 minutes. (If you find that the soup is too thick, add a bit more water; if it's too watery, add a few more noodles or two or three pieces of cubed white bread with the crusts trimmed off.)

Season to taste with salt and pepper and serve hot with a salad and crusty bread.

FRIENDSHIP JOURNAL

This lovely keepsake can be used to chronicle the many special dates, special days, and special events you share with your good friends.

MATERIALS

½ yard of 34-inch-wide fabric (cotton or polyester, but make sure the fabric isn't too heavy; calico is ideal)

1 pair scissors

2 pieces heavy-duty cardboard approximately 8 by 10 inches

1 bottle fabric glue

1 hole puncher
25 sheets paper (stationery, construction, or
    other)
18-inch piece of ribbon
1 photograph about 4 by 5 inches
30-inch piece of lace trim

1. Cut two strips
   of fabric 17
   inches long by
   11 inches wide.
2. Place one piece
   of cardboard
   with the 10-inch
   side ½ inch
   inside the width
   of the fabric.
   Run a bead of
   glue along the
   10-inch side of
   the cardboard
   and along the
   ½-inch seam
   allowance of the
   fabric. Fold the
   fabric over the
   edge of the

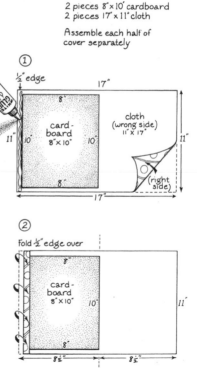

2 pieces 8" x 10" cardboard
2 pieces 17" x 11" cloth

Assemble each half of
cover separately

① ½" edge   17"

8"

cloth
(wrong side)
11" x 17"

card-
board
8" x 10"

11" 10"   10"

8"

(right
side)

17"

② Fold ½" edge over

8"

card-
board
8" x 10"   10"

8"

8½"   8½"

cardboard and hold in place until glue is firmly fixed.

3. Run a bead of glue along 8 inches of each 17-inch side of the fabric and fold it over the edge of the cardboard; hold in place until set. You can use clothespins to clip and hold the seam until the glue dries.

4. Continue the fold along the balance of the fabric and glue the fabric to itself. Run another bead of glue along the opposite 8-inch

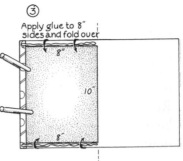

③

Apply glue to 8" sides and fold over

8"

10"

8"

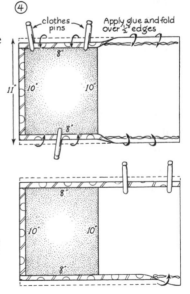

④

clothes pins

Apply glue and fold over ¼" edges

8"

11"

10"

10"

8"

8"

10"

10"

8"

side of the cardboard and pull the fabric tightly across the cardboard.

5. Run another bead of glue down the other 10-inch side of the cover and fold the fabric inward, going ½ inch over the edge, to create the last seam.

6. Fold the ½-inch overhang in on itself. Run a line of glue down the other edge and press together. Repeat the procedure for the other piece of cardboard. Now you have both a

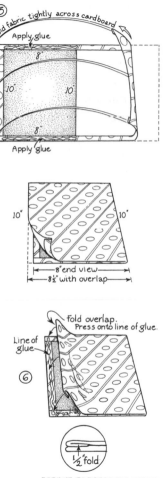

⑤ Fold fabric tightly across cardboard
Apply glue
8"
10" 10"
8"
Apply glue

10" 10"
8" end view
8¼" with overlap

fold overlap.
Press onto line of glue.
Line of glue
⑥

½" fold

REPEAT PROCESS FOR OTHER
HALF OF JOURNAL COVER.

99

top and a bottom cover.

7. Using a sheet of loose-leaf paper for measuring, mark evenly spaced holes for punching. Make sure the holes match up on each half of the cover. Use a hole puncher to make the holes.

8. Using the loose-leaf paper again, mark the hole locations on your chosen journal paper. Make sure the holes line up with the holes in the cover. Use the hole puncher.

9. Place the pieces of two-holed

⑦ Mark 2 holes with a pencil, on each half of the cover.

These holes must align.

Top cover

Bottom cover

Use a nail to make holes in each cover.

⑧ Using the looseleaf paper again as a guide mark hole locations on your chosen journal paper. Then use a hole punch or pointed tool to make holes.

Hole punch

100

paper you have made inside the journal and draw the ribbon up through the holes: Insert one edge of the ribbon through one hole, coming from the bottom to the top, and the opposite edge through the other hole, from the bottom up. You should have both ends on the top of the cover, which should now be tied into a nice bow.

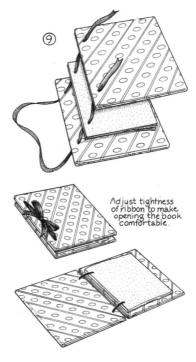

⑨

Adjust tightness of ribbon to make opening the book comfortable.

10. Glue the photograph of your choice onto the center of the top cover. Decorate the

edges with
lace that
you glue
down.

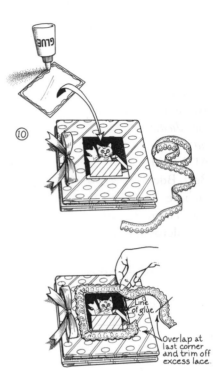

Use the journal to record your friends' birth dates, to glue in their photos, or to have them write down their thoughts on special occasions.

ABOUT THE AUTHOR OF
PORTRAITS OF LITTLE WOMEN

SUSAN BETH PFEFFER is the author of both middle-grade and young adult fiction. Her middle-grade novels include *Nobody's Daughter* and its companion, *Justice for Emily*. Her highly praised *The Year Without Michael* is an ALA Best Book for Young Adults, an ALA YALSA Best of the Best, and a *Publishers Weekly* Best Book of the Year. Her novels for young adults include *Twice Taken, Most Precious Blood, About David,* and *Family of Strangers*. Susan Beth Pfeffer lives in Middletown, New York.

A WORD ABOUT
LOUISA MAY ALCOTT

LOUISA MAY ALCOTT was born in 1832 in Germantown, Pennsylvania, and grew up in the Boston-Concord area of Massachusetts. She received her early education from her father, Bronson Alcott, a renowned educator and writer, who eventually left teaching to study philosophy. To supplement the family income, Louisa worked as a teacher, a household servant, and a seamstress, and she wrote stories as well as poems for newspapers and magazines. In 1868 she published the first volume of *Little Women,* a novel about four sisters growing up in a small New England town during the Civil War. The immediate success of *Little Women* made Louisa May Alcott a celebrated writer, and the novel remains one of today's best-loved books. Alcott wrote until her death in 1888.